P9-DWS-586

PJ Masks Save the Library!

Based on the episode
"Owlette and the Flash Flip Trip"

Ready-to-Read

Simon Spotlight
New York London Toronto Sydney New Delhi

SIMON SPOTLIGHT
An imprint of Simon & Schuster Children's Publishing Division
1230 Avenue of the Americas, New York, New York 10020
This Simon Spotlight edition December 2016
Adapted by Daphne Pendergrass from the series PJ Masks
This book is based on the TV series PJ MASKS © Frog Box / Entertainment One UK
Limited / Walt Disney EMEA Productions Limited 2014
Les Pyjamasques by Romuald © (2007) Gallimard Jeunesse. All Rights Reserved.
This book/publication © Entertainment One UK Limited 2016.
For information about special discounts for bulk purchases, please contact
Simon & Schuster Special Sales at 1-866-506-1949 or business@simonandschuster.com.
Manufactured in the United States of America 1116 LAK
10 9 8 7 6 5 4 3 2 1
ISBN 978-1-4814-8893-8 (hc)
ISBN 978-1-4814-8892-1 (pbk)
ISBN 978-1-4814-8894-5 (eBook)

Amaya is excited to read her Flossy Flash superhero book.

Oh no! Someone erased all the stories! The books just have pictures of Romeo inside!

This looks like a job
for the PJ Masks!

Greg becomes Gekko!

Connor becomes Catboy!

Amaya becomes Owlette!

They are the
PJ Masks!

Owlette is reading
her Flossy Flash book.

She wants to be
like Flossy Flash.

In the Cat-Car,
Catboy asks Owlette
to use her Owl Eyes
to find Romeo.

Owlette wants powers

like Flossy Flash instead.

Catboy hears Romeo
with his Super Cat Ears.

Oh no! Romeo ruined more books and is escaping!

"Where will Romeo go next?" Catboy asks.

"To the library!"

Gekko shouts.

"We have to stop him!"

The heroes make a plan.
Gekko climbs high with
his Super Lizard Grip.

He asks Owlette to look
for Romeo with her
Owl Eyes.

Instead, she pretends to
be Flossy Flash!

She forgets to look
for Romeo!

"Robot!" Owlette cries
when she sees Romeo and
his robot.

Owlette is too late.

Romeo ties up

Gekko and Catboy!

"I will save you with
my Flossy Flash Flip!"
Owlette says.

Owlette trips and falls.

Romeo laughs and steals

all the library books!

"I should have used
my owl powers,"
Owlette says.

"Time to be a hero!"
she says. She sets
Catboy and Gekko free.

She uses her Owl Eyes
and Super Owl Wings
to look for Romeo.

She sees Romeo.

"I still have my book!"
she shouts.

Romeo and his robot

chase her!

Catboy and Gekko

tie up the robot!

The PJ Masks fix all
the books.

They save the library!